SAMANTHA
The Snob

Samantha

The Snob

Jenny Oldfield

Illustrated by Kate Aldous

Hodder
Children's
Books

a division of Hodder Headline Limited

With special thanks to the children of Gisburn Road County
Primary School, Barnoldswick and Archbishop of York
Church of England School, Bishopsthorpe

Copyright © 1999 Jenny Oldfield
Illustrations copyright © 1999 Kate Aldous

First published in Great Britain in 1999
by Hodder Children's Books

A Catalogue record for this book is available from the British Library

ISBN 0 340 74681 5

Typeset by Avon Dataset Ltd, Bidford-on-Avon, Warks

Printed and bound in Great Britain by
The Guernsey Press Co. Ltd, Guernsey, Channel Isles

Hodder Children's Books
a division of Hodder Headline Limited
338 Euston Road
London NW1 3BH

One

'Freedom!' Helen Moore cried. '*F-f-free-ee-dom*!'

Her twin sister, Hannah, ran up the hill to their house, Home Farm. 'No more school for two whole weeks! No more school for two whole weeks!' she chanted over and over.

Whizz – thump! A snowball hit Helen between the shoulder blades. 'Hey!' She spun round just in time to spot their neighbour, Sam Lawson, bob down behind a wall.

'No more school . . . no more school!' Hannah chugged on through the snow.

Whizz – thump! This time the missile landed

smack on the back of Hannah's head.

'It's Sam. Let's get him!' Helen hissed.

Hannah hesitated. 'Do we have to? It's too cold. I want to get home,' she objected.

'Wimp!' Helen decided to go after the enemy on a solo mission. Jumping knee-deep into a drift at the side of the road, she scrambled across the ditch and over the wall into Fred Hunt's field.

Sam was crouched beside the wall about ten metres away. He was too busy stockpiling snowballs to notice what Helen was doing. So she scraped a handful of snow off the wall-top, clamped it between the palms of her gloved hands into a rough sphere (no high-tech missile technology for Helen Moore), then launched it at the enemy before he had a chance to look round.

Lob – plop! The so-called snowball fell two metres short.

'What was that?' Sam yelled derisively, swinging round and launching a volley of compact, icy ammunition.

Whizz – whizz – whizz! Thud – smack – thump!

Helen crouched and put up both arms to shield her head. The snowballs landed on target and slid icily into the gap between her woollen scarf and the collar of her padded jacket, down the back of her neck.

'Crackpot Farm three – Home Farm nil!' Sam crowed.

But he spoke too soon. Hannah was standing on top of the wall with a stack of snowballs. She threw them in quick succession, arms whirling, smacking them into Sam's undefended figure. 'Crackpot Farm three – Home Farm five!' she cried.

'You're soaked!' their dad said as they kicked off their boots at the kitchen door and drip-dripped their way across to the table.

'Yeah. But if you think we're wet, you should see Sam Lawson!' Helen sighed happily, wriggling her cold toes inside the soggiest pair of socks ever.

'What's for tea, Dad?' Hannah flopped into the chair nearest to the warm stove.

'Tea? Now, let's see . . .' David Moore pretended to rattle empty boxes and tins on a shelf in the corner. 'Cupboard's bare, I'm afraid.'

'How come?' Grabbing Socks the cat from another chair, Helen plonked herself down. She felt Speckle their Border collie come and settle under the table, cosying up against her poor cold feet.

Their dad strolled to the window and made one of his big, sweeping arm gestures. 'Outside on Doveton Fell . . . snow . . . big white flakes coming down from cloudy sky . . . freezing cold . . . Or didn't you notice?'

'Yeah, yeah!' Helen stroked Socks and yawned. 'So?'

'So . . . snowstorm . . . Mum stuck over in Nesfield with car load of groceries . . . hence Mother Hubbard situation here at Home Farm.' David went and picked up the girls' schoolbags from the floor. 'Wet – wet – wet!' he moaned.

'Dad, don't squash them!' Hannah leaped from her seat as she saw him dump the bags on the draining-board.

'Too late. They already look as if they've been steamrollered, not to mention plunged into an icy stream. Whatever have you got inside?'

'End of term treat!' Hannah gasped. 'Miss Wesley let us bring it home . . .'

'Oh no, not the school gerbil!' David's voice took on a mock-tragic tone. 'Geoffrey the gerbil, flattened in transit. The *ex*-school gerbil. Or should that be the school *ex*-gerbil?'

'Da-ad!' Pushing him out of the way, Hannah tore open her bag and pulled out . . . a piece of chewed-up, screwed-up, sopping-wet cardboard.

'What,' said their dad, 'is that?'

Hannah held up the sorry object. It had pieces of tinsel hanging from it, shreds of pink crepe paper, a crooked stick with a crumpled silver star. 'It's the fairy from the top of the school tree,' she frowned.

'*Was*!' Helen corrected. 'It *was* the fairy from the top of the tree!'

'Well, Happy Christmas!' David sighed.

It was eight o'clock and still snowing. The twins' mother, Mary, had phoned to say she would have to stay the night at a Bed and Breakfast place close to the Curlew, the cafe she ran in Nesfield.

'But we'll starve!' Helen had protested. 'Dad says it's Mother Hubbard, bare cupboard, no bones for the poor dog!'

'Rubbish!' her mum had replied. 'Your dad's exaggerating as usual.'

'. . . Mum says you're exaggerating as usual!' Helen

had reported back. She'd looked in the freezer and found stacks of food. She'd chosen homemade veggie soup, followed by frozen, homemade shepherds' pie, topped off with apple strudel (homemade).

She and Hannah had helped their dad to prepare supper and allowed him one glass of red wine to go with the meal.

'Two?' he'd begged.

'Da-ad!' they'd warned in chorus.

'You girls sound more and more like your mother with every day that passes!' he'd sulked.

They'd relented at last and Hannah had just poured him a second glass.

So, 'Cheers! Happy Christmas!' he said now, feet up in front of the TV.

'*Freedom*!' Helen sang to a tune she'd made up. She tickled Speckle's tum and scratched behind his ears as they lay side by side on the front-room rug. '*F-f-fre-ee-dom, oh yeah*!'

'Dad, could you turn the TV down? I'm trying to read.' Hannah had her nose buried deep in a large, heavy book.

On the small screen, a Hollywood filmstar with a short haircut was climbing up a mountain with a bunch of kids dressed in gathered skirts and leather shorts. She was singing that the hills were alive with the sound of music. Between her and Helen's tuneless drone, Hannah found that she just couldn't concentrate.

'*Wotcha* reading?' Helen broke off from singing and came to peek at the book title. '*Two Weeks to a Perfectly Trained Dog*. Hmm.'

'Dad, tell Helen not to say "hmm" like that!' Hannah snatched the book away.

'Hmm?' He paid not the slightest attention.

'Hah!' Helen made a grab for the weighty manual. ' "Never *force* your dog to obey your command," ' she read out loud. ' "Always wait until the desired behaviour occurs naturally." Yeah!'

Hannah grabbed it back. 'It's called op – operant conditioning,' she insisted, re-reading the introduction. 'It means never punishing, always praising and rewarding for good behaviour.'

Helen's eyes lit up. 'You hear that, Dad; this book says never punish your children or your dogs!'

'Hmm.' The latest song on TV about a yodelling goatherd had sent him into a light snooze.

'So why are you reading about it?' Helen wanted

7

to know, returning to the rug and Speckle. 'We already have the perfect pooch, don't we, Speckle?'

The Border collie rolled on to his back for more tickling.

'Well, you know we've got two weeks' holiday?' Hannah browsed on through the next page. 'I thought we could put Speckle on the Advanced Training Programme, which takes exactly fourteen days; at the end of which, Speckle would be ready for any kind of Obedience Trials you can think of!'

Helen yawned again., 'Speckle already *has* a degree in obedience; watch.'

Kneeling up, she called the dog's name. 'Sit, Speckle!'

He sat.

'Lie down, Speckle!'

The black and white dog lay down.

'Stay!'

He stayed.

'See!' Helen spread her palms wide. Case proven.

'But you're doing it all wrong,' Hannah frowned. 'You're not supposed to use his name for commands to do with staying in one place; only for ones where you want him to move. It says so in this book!'

'Well, sorry. It just so happens that Speckle didn't read your precious book!'

Sighing and snapping the library book shut, Hannah gave up with bad grace. 'I just thought it was a good idea, that's all!' she said huffily as she gathered her belongings, ready to head upstairs. 'Something useful to do over Christmas, instead of stuffing ourselves with turkey and pud.'

'Uh-huh? Who mentioned turkey?' David Moore woke up with a start.

'I did. Never mind.' Hannah made her exit with a frown and a flounce.

Her dad peered round the room at Helen and Speckle. 'What happened? Where's Hannah going?'

'Bed.'

'Bed? Without being told?' He sat up straight, hair ruffled, shirt crumpled. 'What's wrong? Is she ill? Hannah, come back . . .'

'Sorry!' Helen ran alongside Hannah, who strode down the lane in silence. 'Sorry – sorry – so-rry!'

It was early Saturday morning, the first real day of the holiday. Snow covered the Fell in a smooth white layer under a clear blue sky. Hannah had set off with Speckle to see Laura Saunders at Doveton Manor without even telling Helen where she was going.

'I didn't mean to upset you. Obedience training could be a good idea for Speckle!' Helen had pulled on her boots and zipped up her jacket, then run out of the house to catch them up.

'You're only saying that!' Hannah grunted. 'You don't mean it.'

Crunch – crunch – crunch went their feet over the crisp snow. *Whizz – thud*! A snowball flew wide of the twins and hit Speckle's tail. The dog whirled round and barked.

'Sam!' Hannah and Helen cried. Forgetting their quarrel, they scooped up snow, diving across the ditch and pelting the figure crouched behind the wall. Speckle joined in by leaping the wall and charging the old enemy.

'Hey, three against one; not fair!' Sam protested.

'Yeah!' Hannah and Helen laughed, pelting him without mercy.

They scored an easy victory and walked on.

'So, about this special dog-training programme,' Hannah began again as the wide gateway to Doveton

Manor came into view. The Saunderses' house sat well back from the road, behind smooth lawns and terraces. 'We could start Speckle on it this afternoon. All we need is a rolled-up newspaper and a jumping-stick . . .'

Woof – woo-ooff – woof!

Her description of the operant conditioning method was rudely interrupted.

A black and tan bundle of fur sprang out from behind the stone gatepost. All floppy ears and furry paws, the small spaniel flung itself at Speckle.

'Heel, Speckle!' Helen cried.

The Border collie responded immediately. He tucked himself out of the way while the little dog barked and yapped.

'It's gone berserk!' Hannah hissed, looking up and down the drive for an owner. The Saunderses had horses and a cat, but no dog, she knew.

Wooff – yap – woo-oof! The spaniel hurled itself around Helen's legs and flew at Speckle. Its teeth and gums were bared, its ears flapping in front of its big brown eyes.

'Samantha!' a voice called. 'Come here at once!'

'No chance!' Helen muttered as the strange dog

11

ignored her owner. Samantha had set her sights on sinking those pearly white teeth into Speckle. So Helen tried to stand her ground in-between the two dogs, hoping that the owner would pull the spaniel off before any damage was done.

'Hold on to your dog!' After the strange, vicious little dog came a large and distressed-looking owner. The woman ploughed across the snowy lawn without coat or boots, floundering up to her knees. Her cropped hair was as white as the snow, her cheeks red and flustered.

Obligingly Hannah bent to take hold of Speckle's collar. Meanwhile, Samantha the spaniel had taken hold of one leg of Helen's jeans and was wrestling and snarling in a flurry of churned up snow.

'Samantha!' The woman arrived at last and made a lunge for her dog. She missed, tried again and missed.

Helen shook her leg to try to free herself. No good. The spaniel clung on tight.

'Samantha, darling, *do* be good!' the woman pleaded, huffing and puffing after her struggle across the lawn.

Wrrr – grrr – rrrrgh! The spaniel's jaws were still

clamped to Helen's trousers.

Then Hannah saw Laura Saunders running down the drive, her fair hair flying free, a look of concern on her face as she arrived and took in the scene.

Speckle sat obediently to heel at Helen's side. One large lady was pleading with one small dog to let go of Helen's jeans. One small dog ignored one large lady.

'Hi, Hannah, hi, Helen,' Laura sighed with an embarrassed grin. 'I'd like you to meet our Christmas guests. This is Lady Caroline Urquhart and her spaniel, Samantha-Henrietta-Tansy of Fife.'

Two

'Lady Caroline *Erk-utt*?' Hannah thought that Laura must have coughed and choked on the dog's owner's name. She stretched the corners of her mouth in a downwards grimace and rolled her eyes at Helen.

'*Gerroff*!' Helen cried. She shook her leg to free herself from Samantha-Henrietta-Something-Something's vice-like jaws.

'Sammie, darling!' Lady Caroline wailed ineffectively. 'Let go of the little girl's trousers!'

Wrrr – rrr – grrrufff! Samantha the spaniel held on tight.

'Who'd have thought that such a small dog could

be so strong?' Hannah mused, as she watched Helen fail to detach herself from the pesky pooch. Helen raised her leg and lifted Samantha clear of the ground, jaws still clamped firmly to her jeans.

'Never mind that! Just help, OK?' Helen hissed.

'Now *there's* someone who could benefit from the Two Weeks to a Perfectly Trained Dog programme!' Hannah went on with a bright smile. Then she whispered to Speckle to move out of harm's way.

The Border collie obligingly shifted position as Helen and Samantha struggled on.

'Help!' Helen cried.

Grrrr – rurrgh!

'Down, Samantha!' Lady C made a wildly inaccurate lunge, scooping up only snow. 'Please do as Mummy says!'

As if! Hannah thought.

'Help!' Helen waved her arms windmill-fashion, overbalanced, toppled and landed in a laurel bush loaded with snow.

Yip! Just in time to escape the shower of wet snow being dumped on her pretty head, Samantha yelped and let go. In a flurry of black and brown fur she leaped for the safety of her owner's arms.

'Oh, Helen, sorry!' Laura rushed to pull her out of the bush. 'Samantha only arrived here last night. She hasn't had time to settle down properly yet!'

'Don't worry. It's all right,' Helen muttered, brushing snow out of crevices in her trousers.

Laura helped. 'Did she get your leg?'

'No, just my jeans.' She spotted a row of small round holes in the denim, where the spaniel's teeth had pierced the cloth. 'Grrr-eat!'

'You sound like a dog!' Hannah remarked. She still hadn't forgiven Helen for the Advanced Training episode. Turning to Laura's visitor, she began to ask polite questions. 'What sort of spaniel is Samantha exactly?'

'She's a Cavalier King Charles.' Lady Caroline hugged her tiny dog to her large chest. Her voice rose and fell, and she rolled her 'r's with a Scottish accent which Helen found hard to understand at first. 'The breed is descended from the toy spaniel of the sixteenth century. You can tell the Cavalier apart from the King Charles proper by the shape of the skull and nose. Cavaliers have longer noses and flatter heads than the Charlies, and they're a little larger. Aren't you, darling?'

'She's sweet!' Hannah admitted, now that Samantha had snuggled into Lady C's arms. The tiny dog was mostly black, with bright tan fur around her nose, chest and paws. Her ears were long and floppy, her eyes round and nut-brown.

'Sweet!' Helen exploded in the background.

'Shh!' Laura warned her not to upset their guest.

'What's her full name again?' Hannah went on.

'Samantha-Henrietta-Tansy of Fife.' Lady Caroline repeated the mouthful slowly. 'Henrietta after the wife of Charles the Second, Tansy because she's a pure-bred black and tan. Tan – Tansy, you see.'

'And why Fife?' Hannah asked, walking up the snowy drive with dog and owner. Privately she was wondering how long the *Erk-utts* might be staying at the manor. Two weeks perhaps . . . ?

'Fife is the county in Scotland where we live,' the Saunderses' house guest explained.

They went up on to the terrace, past the frozen fish-pond, around the side of the big house. In the kitchen, Helen could see Laura's mother, Valerie Saunders, putting finishing touches to the white icing on this year's Christmas cake.

Samantha too spotted the warmth and comfort of

the kitchen. So she launched straight into what Helen would later describe to her dad as 'The Worst Dog in the World Routine'.

First, she opened her mouth and nipped Lady Caroline's plump hand with her sharp white teeth.

('Those same little fangs that had already perforated my jeans!' Helen said later.)

Then, as her owner gasped, she bounded free. She sped across the terrace and through the kitchen door.

('Oh no!' David Moore guessed what happened next. 'Not the Christmas cake!')

Samantha saw another pair of legs to grab, and smelt the cake.

'Ouch!' Valerie Saunders felt the nip of those incisors. She stepped smartly away from the table, leaving the coast clear for the spaniel to make a mighty leap.

('Unbelievable!' Hannah told her dad. 'She jumped *this high* from a standing start!')

She took a chunk out of the beautiful white cake, then legged it across the table and down the other side, mouth full of a delicious, sugary treat. Then she was scooting over the polished red tiles, chasing

Lady, the Saunderses' elegant Siamese cat, through the door, across the wide hall into the lounge, where she scattered crumbs and trailed dirty wet footprints across the beige carpet.

(*Beige* carpet!' David Moore shook his head and pointed out that the pale colour was always a big mistake as far as carpets went.)

Worse, the Saunderses' sofa was cream silk. Cream and very expensive. Samantha leaped up and tramped from cushion to cushion. She trod cake currants into the shiny surface and ignored Laura's frantic attempts to pull her off.

'Down, Samantha!' Lady Caroline cried weakly.

Give me two weeks with that dog and I could get her to behave perfectly! Hannah said to herself with grim determination.

Then, when Samantha-Henrietta-Tansy of Fife was puffed and out of breath from the chase, she simply jumped from the sofa and plumped down on a deep red cushion with gold tassels which had been set out for her beside the roaring log fire.

Tight-lipped, Valerie Saunders brought a damp cloth and wiped at the paw marks on her cream silk sofa. Lady Caroline wagged her stubby finger at the spaniel. Laura, Hannah and Helen gathered nervously with Speckle in the far corner of the room.

'And you know what was the worst thing of all?' Helen cried to her father.

It was lunchtime. The sun had begun to melt the snow from the roofs of the barn and house at Home Farm, so that the twins' account of Samantha's exploits was accompanied by a steady drip-drip-drip from the ancient gutters.

'Now let me see, the worst thing . . . ?' David was stirring soup and keeping an eye on bread toasting in the toaster. 'That would be taking a chunk out of the Christmas cake, wouldn't it?'

'No!' Helen's wide stare told him this was very serious.

'Well then, the worst thing would be ruining Valerie's posh sofa.' He cleared his throat and tried not to smile.

'No!'

'Biting her ankle?'

'No!'

'What then?' He set the food on the table and took spoons from the drawer.

'The worst thing was how Samantha treated Speckle!' Helen told him. Ignoring her soup, she dropped to her knees to pet and stroke the collie.

David glanced at Hannah, who gave a quiet nod.

'Why, what did she do?' he asked her.

Hannah sighed. She didn't like to criticise any animal; after all, their bad behaviour was usually down to their owner.

But Helen jumped in with the answer. 'She only ignored Speckle!'

David's eyes widened. 'How do you mean?'

'Samantha sits on this red velvet cushion that Lady

Caroline's brought along specially from their castle in Scotland . . .'

'Castle in Scotland!' her dad echoed with a low whistle. 'Wow!'

'. . . So, the stupid little spaniel is sitting there with her nose in the air, and Speckle comes along all friendly as usual.' Helen's voice rose as she recalled the scene. 'His tail's wagging and his ears are pricked. He's saying "Hello, I'm your friendly neighbour. I live on a farm just up the hill!" '

'That's right.' Hannah's sighs deepened. 'Samantha wasn't very nice.'

'*Not very nice*!' Helen didn't think this went nearly far enough. 'What does Samantha do when Speckle says hello? She looks at him down her nose like this! (Squinting down the length of her turned-up nose.) She turns her head away like she's a real snob and stares at the fire as if Speckle's not there!'

'She ignored him?' David asked to make sure he'd got it right.

'Yeah, she's a snob!' Helen repeated, hugging Speckle hard. 'And she cut our beautiful, lovely, wonderful dog dead!'

Three

'Here comes your mum!' David Moore called from the house.

It was Sunday morning and the twins were in the barn doing winter jobs for their grey pony, Solo. Helen was mixing a scoop of feed with half a scoop of sugar-beet in a yellow plastic bowl. Hannah was unfastening the clips on his rug and lifting it from his broad back, ready to brush him from head to foot.

They heard a car engine in the lane; the first since the weekend snow had set in. It meant the road was clear at last.

So the girls ran outside in time to see the elderly family car struggle up the steep hill. They waited impatiently for their mother to pull up in the yard and step out.

'Hi, Mum!' they cried, flinging their arms around her and checking to see that she was all right.

'Of course I'm OK!' Mary detached herself and laughed. 'I was perfectly safe at the B and B. It wasn't as if I was stuck on the Fell, in danger of dying of exposure or anything.'

'We missed you!' Hannah protested, opening up the boot to lift out a box of supermarket groceries.

'You mean, you missed your chocolate biscuits and packets of crisps!' She pointed out a major reason why they might be glad to see her, then handed Helen a second box.

'Chocolate biscuits! What sort?' Helen demanded, dashing inside with her haul.

'Well, *I* really did miss you,' their dad said, giving her a hug. 'And it's not just cupboard love!'

Hannah curled her lip and rolled her eyes.

'Look away, Hann!' Mary advised as she returned the hug and added a kiss. Then she asked what had been happening since she'd been away.

'We finished school!' Helen dumped her box on the kitchen table and dived for the biscuits.

'We beat Sam in a snowball fight!' Hannah recorded the important victory.

Helen's mouth was already full of chocolate digestive when she pounced on a crumpled pink and silver object behind the TV. 'School angel!' she mumbled. 'Miss Wesley said we could keep it.'

'Very pretty, dear. And before you ask, no, we can't put it on top of our tree in that bedraggled state. What else?'

Handing Mary a mug of coffee, David dragged the subject round to the one the girls had been avoiding. 'Last but not least, we've had a most unusual experience. While you've been snowed up in Nesfield, Helen and Hannah have actually come across an animal they don't get on with. In fact, according to Helen, they've been introduced to the Worst Dog in the World!'

'Dad's exaggerating!' Hannah said quietly, working a soft brush over Solo's neck and shoulders.

They'd taken their mum to the barn to see him before she took her jacket off and now they were getting on with the jobs they'd abandoned when she'd arrived.

'No, he's not!' Helen insisted, unable to forgive the snobbish spaniel for cutting their darling Speckle dead. 'Samantha-*Thingummy* is the horriblest animal!'

Hannah left off brushing and rested her hand on Solo's warm back. 'It's not her fault. It's Lady Caroline *Erk-utt's*.'

'Come again?' Mary stroked the pony's soft grey muzzle.

'Urquhart,' David told them. 'It's Scottish. Spelt U-R-Q-U-H-A-R-T, pronounced *Erkutt*.'

'We know!' Helen and Hannah lied.

'Anyway, Samantha the Snob is visiting Doveton Manor for Christmas,' Helen went on. 'And she's this stupid, black and brown furry thing who's completely out of control!'

'I take it you don't like her?' Crossing her arms, Mary leaned back against the wall and smiled quietly.

'She punctured my new jeans!' Helen pointed out, telling her mum about the episode by the manor gates.

'Yes, if only I could get my hands on her!' Hannah added.

Mary turned in surprise. 'You mean, even you, Hannah; you'd cheerfully strangle the poor little thing?'

'No way!' She began to brush again; smoothly, rhythmically, raising dust from Solo's thick winter coat. 'I'm talking about how I'd train her if I got half the chance.'

Frowning, Helen grabbed a fork and began mucking out Solo's stall. 'Don't listen to her!' she muttered. 'You've heard of the Horse Whisperer, haven't you? Well, Hannah thinks she's the Dog Whisperer!'

'I don't.' With all the quiet confidence of One Who Has Seen the Light, Hannah went on grooming Solo. 'I've read a library book, that's all. It tells you about this fantastic way of training dogs – Op-operant conditioning. It says to praise your pooch, not smack him – ever!'

'And you think it works?' Her mum saw that she was serious and paid attention, in spite of Helen snorting and flinging straw about in Solo's stall.

Hannah brushed until her arm ached. 'Yep.'

'How will you find out?'

'I'm going to try it.'

'Not on Samantha-*Thingummy*?' Mary asked.

'No. On Speckle.' Hannah's eyes met Helen's over Solo's back. She jutted out her chin and put on a defiant tone. 'All I need is a rolled-up newspaper and a jumping-stick. I'm going to start straight after lunch!'

' "Retrieving and Jumping",' Hannah read from the chapter headed 'Advanced Obedience'. Her teeth chattered and her fingers trembled as she tried to hold the heavy book. Alone with Speckle in the yard at Home Farm, she began to wonder whether beginning the training three days before Christmas, with snow still on the ground and a sharp frost forecast for tonight, was such a good idea after all.

'First, roll up your newspaper nice and tight.' – *Done that*! 'Now get your dog to accept the object in his mouth. Say "Take it!" and praise him when he does.' *Hmm, so far so good*! Hannah had no trouble getting Speckle to carry the paper. 'Now press the sides of his mouth to open his jaws, and say "Drop it!" ' *No problem*! Speckle had let go before she'd even said the words. 'Good boy, Speckle!' she murmured, then began all over again.

'What're you up to, if it's not a daft question?' Strolling down the lane on his way to Doveton village, Sam stopped to watch.

'It is,' Hannah said shortly. At this rate, Speckle would be retrieving the roll of newspaper before teatime. Their super-obedient Border collie was going to be no challenge to her new-found training skills.

'If you're teaching him to fetch, you're wasting your time,' Sam scoffed. 'Speckle's a sheepdog; it's bred into them to fetch stuff from the minute they're born!'

'Thank you, Sam!' Hannah said between gritted teeth. Her face turned red in spite of the cold air. No wonder Speckle had been learning so fast. She decided to skip retrieving and move on to jumping.

And luckily Sam had lost interest in what she and Speckle were doing. He'd walked a few yards down the hill and was calling out to someone approaching in the other direction.

'What d'you call that?' he jeered at the newcomer. 'Is it a toy, or what?'

'Of course it's not a toy!' Laura's voice replied. 'It's a real dog!'

Hannah stopped what she was doing and went to the gate. She saw Laura bringing Samantha for a walk on the Fell.

'Call that a real dog!' Sam was enjoying himself, crouching down to the spaniel's level and giving a high-pitched bark.

Samantha bared her teeth and growled.

'Gosh, I'm frightened!' Sam crowed. 'You're a big, fierce, scary monster!'

'I wouldn't do that,' Laura said, holding fast to the little dog's lead. 'Samantha doesn't like you to make fun of her.'

'*Grrr-ruff*!' The twins' neighbour ignored the warning and gave a fake growl.

Samantha strained at the leash, obviously dying to sink her fangs into the boy's leg as he straightened up and walked boldly by. By the time he'd disappeared round the bend and Laura had reached Home Farm, the bad-tempered little dog was in the worst possible mood.

'Hi, Hannah, I hoped I'd see you,' Laura began, raising her voice above Samantha's throaty growl. 'I wanted to say sorry about yesterday.'

'That's OK. It can't be much fun for you either, having Samantha on the rampage at the Manor.'

'It isn't,' Laura agreed. 'But Mum and Dad invited Lady Caroline for Christmas because they feel sorry for her. Her husband just died a few months ago, and she's all by herself in a great big house. They said it would be a horrible Christmas for her if she stayed up in Fife.'

Hannah nodded, aware of Speckle edging forward to say hello to the visitor. Samantha, who was having none of it, kept up her fierce growl. 'How come your

mum and dad know Lady Caroline?' she asked.

'They met her on holiday a few years ago. She doesn't have any family or anything; only Samantha.'

'Who's been spoiled to death,' Hannah concluded.

Laura agreed. 'You know, she's a really picky eater. She only has chicken; nothing else.'

'Except Christmas cake,' Hannah reminded her.

'And chocolate. But Lady Caroline only gives her Belgian chocolates, which are the most expensive kind.' Laura sighed and shook her head as the little dog suddenly darted at Speckle with a sharp bark and a flurry of floppy ears.

Speckle retreated to the safety of the yard.

'Looks like we'd better keep him away from Doveton Manor until your guests leave!' Hannah decided. The more she saw of Samantha, the more she realised what a hopeless case the little dog was. *And no wonder*, she said to herself. *Her ignorant owner doesn't even seem to realise how bad it is for Samantha to be fed chocolates*!

She said goodbye to Laura, who went back down the hill, and ran inside to find Helen.

'. . . Belgian chocolate!' Helen, who was at the kitchen table making star-shaped Christmas cards out of gold paper and a tube of glitter, could hardly believe her ears. 'I've never in my whole life had a Belgian chocolate!'

'My favourite!' Mary cried from the depths of the front-room sofa.

'There's something to add to your Christmas list, girls!' their dad called from the landing at the top of the stairs. He was carrying newly developed film from the bathroom to his dark-room in the attic. 'A lovely big box of Belgian chocolates for your hard-working mum!'

'Yeah, Dad, and I bet I know who'd scoff the lot!' Helen chipped in. She thought for a few seconds, then drew Hannah into a secret conversation. 'Have we got enough money left over from our other presents to buy Mum those chocs?'

Hannah shook her head and sat down next to Helen.

She decided to consult her dog-training bible to plan ahead for Speckle's next lesson on how to jump a jumping-stick. But the book fell open instead at the chapter about un-teaching bad habits. 'Constant barking', she read. And, 'Chewing. Stealing Food. Chasing cars and bikes.'

They were both so busy that neither got up to answer the phone when it rang.

'Helen, get that, will you?' Mary called lazily.

So Helen sighed and half-slipped her feet into her trainers which she'd kicked off under the table. She slopped out into the hall, hoping that the phone would stop ringing before she got there.

But the caller was persistent.

'Hullo?' Helen said grumpily.

'Hannah, it's me, Laura . . .'

'Hi, Laura, this is Helen.' Something in their friend's tone made her jump to attention. 'What's wrong?'

'Listen, Helen; it's Samantha!'

'What about Samantha?' Had the spoiled little dog stuffed herself too full of chocolates, she wondered.

'I brought her for a walk up to Home Farm. Did Hannah tell you?' Without waiting for a reply, Laura rushed on. 'Well, anyway, I was walking back down the lane with her when I did something really stupid!'

Helen frowned. 'Like what?'

'I don't know what I was thinking! I mean, she's never been to Doveton before, so how could I expect her to find her way back to the Manor if she happened to get lost?' Laura jumped frantically from one thought to another without explaining properly. 'The thing is, she doesn't know any of the landmarks. I should never have let her off the lead. Only, I thought she'd stay with me. I never for a second thought she'd take it into her head to chase Fred Hunt's tractor!'

'Slow down,' Helen begged. 'You're telling me that you let Lady Caroline's dog off the lead and that the dog ran off and got lost?'

Hannah came out of the kitchen just in time to hear Helen's version of what had happened. Her jaw dropped and she opened her brown eyes wide.

'Yes,' Laura sighed. 'I looked all over for her before I decided I'd better come home and tell Lady Caroline what I'd done. She practically fainted on the spot!'

'And you're sure you looked everywhere?' Helen quizzed. Somehow, she didn't find the idea of Samantha the Snob getting lost and having to fend for herself for a change all that upsetting. *Do her good*! she thought.

'Absolutely everywhere!' Laura sighed. 'And Lady Caroline's really, really upset because it's going to be dark soon, and Dad says that they've forecast more snow.' She hesitated then plunged on. 'Helen, the reason I'm calling you, even though I know you and Hannah don't exactly get on with Samantha, is to ask will you please, please, *please* help me to find her!'

Four

'What did you tell Laura?' David Moore wanted to know when he came downstairs from his dark-room and heard about the latest crisis. His dark green, cable-knit jumper still smelled of the chemicals he used to develop his films.

'I said I thought Samantha would come back when she was hungry,' Helen said. There were slight frown lines between her eyebrows and she'd pursed her mouth into a tight circle.

Hannah said nothing; she just looked at her feet and shuffled.

'I don't believe I'm hearing this!' their dad

exclaimed. 'You turned down your friend's request for help?'

'. . . Because I think she was over-reacting,' Helen insisted. 'Over-reacting' was a good word. Miss Wesley used it a lot at school.' It meant 'making a fuss', which was what Helen believed Laura was doing over the dreadful Samantha.

David put a stack of photographs down on the table. 'That's not the point! It's obviously important to Laura to find the dog as quickly as possible, and if you put yourselves in her shoes, you'd soon see why.'

'But Samantha's not stupid!' Helen insisted. 'She won't *really* have got lost; she's just hiding to annoy everyone!'

'. . . You hope!' Hannah muttered.

Helen flashed her a reproachful look. 'Dogs have a good sense of direction,' she went on with a raised voice. 'And a fantastic sense of smell! You might not think it to look at her, but Samantha has got spaniel blood. Those dogs can hunt and track through forests, across rivers, up mountains; they do not get lost on a small hill in the Lake District!'

It was just at this moment that Mary Moore tore

herself away from the fire. 'Do I hear a heated family debate?' she said sweetly as she wandered into the kitchen.

David turned, arms outstretched as if appealing for a wicket in a cricket match. 'The girls have just refused to help Laura look for the little Cavalier!'

'*Helen* has,' Hannah reminded him. 'I never said a word.'

'Traitor!' Helen hissed.

'What do you think, Hann?' Her mum wanted to hear every point of view before she added her opinion.

'I don't know. On the one hand, I'm sorry Lady Caroline's upset. But on the other hand, I agree with Helen; dogs are pretty clever about finding their way back home.'

Helen nodded hard. The look she flashed at her dad said, 'See!'

'. . . On the *other* hand . . .' Hannah went on.

'How many hands have you got?' Mary smiled. 'Listen, can I ask you both a question?'

Hannah and Helen nodded.

'If this was about any other animal except the

apparently awful Samantha, what would you be doing right now?'

They knew what she was getting at; the fact that they'd taken a dislike to Lady Caroline's spoiled pet had definitely been part of the reason why they'd said no to Laura's request for help. It made Hannah colour up bright red and even Helen found it hard to meet her mum's gaze.

But before they could frame an answer, the phone rang again. Their dad answered it quickly this time and came back with more news from Doveton Manor. 'That was Laura. They've had to call the doctor for Lady Caroline. Apparently she was so worried about the dog that she's given herself palpitations.'

'What are they?' Hannah asked. Whatever they were, they sounded serious.

'It's when you get out of breath and your heart thumps and you get hot and sweaty and maybe a bit faint,' her dad explained. He'd quietened down and was looking thoughtful. 'It happens when you get really worried.'

'Is it dangerous?' Helen asked.

'It can be if you're elderly, or if your heart is already a bit dodgy.'

'Poor Valerie and Geoffrey,' Mary murmured. 'This must be a real downer for them. If they're not careful, their entire Christmas could be ruined.'

'And all because they were kind enough to invite a lonely old lady to their house for the holiday,' David muttered.

Gradually, through the murmurings and sighings, all eyes became focussed on Helen.

'And what if Samantha really *is* seriously lost up on the Fell?' Hannah voiced her worst fear in a small, shaky voice.

Helen stared from one to the other. They were putting a lot of pressure on her with those looks. '*OK*!' she said at last. 'Let's find the horrid little nuisance, and then maybe I can get on with making my Christmas cards in peace!'

'Let's start with Fred Hunt!' Helen suggested.

She and Hannah were out in the lane with Speckle, well wrapped up in padded jackets, woolly hats and gloves. It was three o'clock in the afternoon, with only one hour of daylight left. The temperature had dropped below zero, but as yet there was no sign of the snow that had been forecast.

'Why him?' Hannah asked.

'Because Laura happened to mention that Samantha tried to chase his tractor when she let him off the lead. So Fred might have seen which way the pesky dog went.' Helen still couldn't bring herself to be nice about the missing spaniel. She wanted Hannah to know that she was out here in the freezing cold against her better judgment. *Wild goose chase, waste of time* . . . but those three pairs of eyes boring into her had forced her to give in.

They approached High Hartwell by a stile over the stone wall into the farmyard. A strong, sweet smell of cattle came from the large barn as they squeezed between Fred's big yellow tractor and a stack of logs outside the farmhouse door.

The door opened before they had time to knock. 'This isn't about that dog that's run away from the woman at Doveton Manor, is it?' Fred Hunt snapped.

Taken aback, Helen took a deep breath. 'How did you know?'

'Because I've had Laura Saunders on the phone, bending my ear, that's how.' The farmer's stocky figure blocked the doorway as he stood frowning

down at Hannah and Helen. 'I told her I've no idea
what happened to the daft little tyke after it attacked
my tractor tyres. I also said that for two pins I'd
have run it over!'

Ouch! Hannah grimaced.

'A dog like that's no good to man nor beast.' Fred
grumbled on, letting a smell of toasted teacakes waft
out of his door and tickle the twins' noses. 'It's too
small to do anything useful, and besides, that Lady
So-and-so has completely ruined it.'

'Yes,' Helen sighed. Her mouth watered with the
hot, buttered-toast smell.

'So you didn't see where Samantha ran off to?' Hannah quizzed gently.

The old man frowned and shook his head. 'I was driving the tractor into the yard when this little scrap of a spaniel came flying down the lane. I had to put the brakes on fast, I can tell you!'

'Yes, and then afterwards?'

Instead of answering, Fred stooped to pat Speckle on the head, then fished in his tweed jacket pocket for a bone-shaped biscuit. He fed the treat to the politely waiting dog. 'Now *there's* a real useful, well-trained animal,' he murmured.

Hannah grinned. 'I'm teaching him to jump a stick!' she told Fred proudly.

'Speckle will learn that, no problem.' There was a pause, while the farmer considered. 'But why bother? What good will it do?'

'Exactly!' Helen agreed, as if that's what she'd been saying all along. She was getting cold standing here on Fred Hunt's doorstep. 'Mr Hunt, could you possibly tell us which way Samantha ran off after she'd chased your tractor?'

'Well, yes, now you ask, I possibly could!' he teased. 'Let's see. She came down the lane, yap-yap-

yap. She darted at the right-hand tyre. I put on the brakes. She swerved wide of the wheel and round the back of the tractor. That was when Laura Saunders came on the scene, calling for the dog to stop.'

'But Samantha didn't stop?' Hannah prompted.

'She didn't take a blind bit of notice. By this time she was scooting through the gate and across the farmyard towards this very door where we're standing now.'

'And?' Helen urged.

'The door was shut, so the spaniel changed tack again and shot off round the side of the house, going hell-for-leather in the direction of Crackpot Farm.'

'Oh no!' Hannah groaned. *Not Crackpot Farm*!

'Are you sure?' Helen asked. The Lawsons' place stood higher up the hill, which meant that Samantha must have doubled back across country.

'Yes, I'm sure. But you know you'd be wasting your time going up there asking your questions, don't you?'

'No, why?' Helen couldn't work out why he should say this.

Fred Hunt glanced over his shoulder at his teacakes

and mug of hot tea.' 'You're too slow to catch cold today!' he said, already stepping back to close the door on them. 'The first thing Laura Saunders did after she left here was to go up and knock on Sam Lawson's door!'

Five

Helen thought of herself and Hannah as ace-detectives as far as tracing missing animals was concerned. She didn't like the thought that they'd been caught napping.

'Fred's right,' Hannah admitted. 'We should've known that Laura would follow Samantha's trail while it was still warm. What we should *really* be doing now is going straight down to Doveton Manor.'

'To team up with Laura?' Helen nodded, and together they quickened their pace down the lane, Speckle trotting along behind.

'I only hope we don't bump into Lady Caroline.'

Hannah's cheeks tingled in the cold wind. Despite her warm clothes, she couldn't feel either her fingers on her toes.

'Me too.' Helen didn't fancy having to face up to the Saunderses' guest and her 'palpitations'.

They walked in silence, trying to put themselves in the little Cavalier King Charles spaniel's place. They pictured the scene; one small dog charging at one giant tractor in a strange farmyard. A yard full of smells – cows, trampled snow, diesel fumes. And a vast expanse of open hillside beyond.

Samantha might be a spoiled wimp, but she seemed to have plenty of energy and being on the run from Laura was obviously her idea of fun. She must have scampered across the wintry fields, plunging into drifts, her ears caked with frozen snow, her high bark breaking the Sunday silence. When she came to the Lawsons' farm, what then?

It was the answer to this big question that Hannah and Helen would find out from Laura. They found they picked up speed as they reached the main road, and by the time the manor house came into sight they were practically running up to its wide front door. They rang the bell, warm now inside their jackets and scarves, their breath coming out in clouds of steam.

Laura herself opened the door. 'Thank heavens!' she sighed when she saw them, gratefully ushering them into the hall which was festooned with swags of fake pine-branches intertwined with red and gold ribbon and silver balls. A Christmas tree stood in one corner, its fairy lights twinkling. She quickly signalled for them not to make a noise.

'Sorry it took us so long to get here,' Hannah gasped. The Saunderses' central-heating was working overtime, so that the twins were greeted by a blast of hot air. Inside their thick jackets they began to glow and sweat. 'We called at High Hartwell to talk to Fred Hunt.'

'Waste of time,' another voice said.

Helen and Hannah spun round to find Sam Lawson standing there in a blue fleece, jeans and a massive pair of thick, red and white football socks.

He met their surprised stares with a wide grin. 'I said I'd help Laura find her spaniel, didn't I?'

'Why? Is Lady Caroline offering a big reward?' Helen muttered. She was sure that only money could have persuaded Sam Lawson to volunteer.

'Shh!' Laura dug Helen with her elbow and pointed up the wide, curving staircase. Then she drew them all into a sitting-room overlooking the terrace. 'The doctor said she should try to rest.'

Arms folded, striped stockinged feet planted wide apart, Sam pretended to be offended. 'Well, thanks very much, Helen! I don't suppose it's possible that I wanted to help find Samantha without any money being involved!'

'But you called her a pesky—'

'Shh!' This time it was Hannah giving Helen a dig. 'This won't get us anywhere. Sam, I take it you didn't see which way the dog went after she came to your place?'

He shook his head. 'That's just it. One minute she was there, jumping up and making a fuss. Next minute, she'd vanished. Just like that!' Snapping his fingers, Sam made it clear that Samantha's disappearance was a mystery.

'I've already asked him the same question,' Laura cut in, pacing nervously around the room and stepping over the missing Cavalier's empty red velvet cushion. 'And I came to the same dead-end. That was when Sam agreed to help and we decided it would be best to come back to my house, in case Samantha had managed to make her way down from the Fell.'

'But she hadn't.' Helen stated the obvious.

'No. And then I had to confess to Lady Caroline what I'd done.' Laura stopped by the window and looked out across the grounds to the frozen shore of Doveton Lake. She sighed at the memory.

'The old lady went off her head!' Sam hissed, then began to mimic Lady Caroline's voice. ' "You've lost my little darling! Oh, Samantha, come back to Mummy!" '

'Be quiet!' Helen warned, closing the door behind her. She looked down at Speckle and imagined how it would feel to lose him. It would be like a big hole opening up under your feet. Panic. Nightmare.

'I thought she was going to faint,' Laura whispered. 'It's because Samantha's the only thing in the world that means anything to her since Sir Anthony died. And she's convinced that now she's going to lose her pet too.'

'Well, she's not,' Hannah said firmly. 'A dog can't just vanish. Even a small one.' She thought hard, turning to Sam again. 'Go back over it one more time.

What made you realise Samantha was there in the first place? Can you remember?'

'Yes, Miss; no, Miss!' Sam stood to attention with a smirk, then decided to be serious. 'OK. My mum was getting ready to go and see my gran in Nesfield. She wanted me to carry some Christmas stuff out to the car; you know, presents and food that she'd promised to take. There was a bit of a flap because she was late and Gran always worries if she doesn't get there when she says she will.'

Hannah nodded sympathetically. The last-minute rush sounded all too familiar.

'So Mum was running round like a scalded cat looking for her keys and I was loading the car. Then there was this – *thing* grabbing my ankle, snarling and growling and hanging on for grim death!'

'Sounds like Samantha!' Helen sighed at the memory.

'I knew who she belonged to because I'd only just seen her and Laura in the lane a few minutes earlier.'

'Anyway, I showed up while Samantha was still attached to Sam's leg,' Laura explained. 'We were both trying to calm her down and recapture her when Mrs Lawson came out and panicked.'

'My mum panicking is not a pretty sight.' Sam took up the story once more. 'She sees what she thinks is a vicious monster gnawing her little boy's ankle and she launches herself at it with words which I couldn't repeat . . .'

Hannah grinned quickly at Helen. 'Mrs Lawson *over-reacted*!' she giggled.

'She's still yelling and shouting when she tries a rugby tackle,' Sam went on. 'Only, she's not quite that graceful. *Whoomph*! She dives, misses and lands in a heap of snow. Samantha sees this heavy object toppling to the ground and thinks it's time she got out. So she lets go of my leg.'

'Then *I* pounced,' Laura gabbled. 'And she's a wriggly little thing, so I missed too. Sam had to pick his mum up, and I was face-down grabbing thin air. When we all got up and looked around the yard, there was no sign of Samantha!'

Helen frowned. It seemed they were back to square one. But Hannah hadn't finished. 'And what did your mum do next, Sam?'

'You should join the police when you leave school!' he muttered.

'She made sure Sam was OK, then got in her car and drove off to Nesfield,' Laura told her.

'And there was absolutely no sign of Samantha?' Hannah checked.

'We looked everywhere! We checked for paw marks in the snow; everything!'

'Hmm.' Hannah knitted her brows. 'What was in the parcels that your mum had wrapped for your gran?'

Laura, Sam and Helen grunted in surprise. '*Huh*?'

'Where did that question come from?' Sam wanted to know.

Hannah wasn't about to be put off. 'Just tell me, please,' she said calmly in her best Sherlock Holmes voice. 'Was one of the presents a nice big box of chocolates by any chance?'

'Chocolates – Samantha's favourite doggy treat!' Helen was trying to explain in easy stages as Hannah picked up the phone and dialled the number that Sam had given her.

Light was dawning on her listeners' faces.

'Especially Belgian,' Helen added.

Sam's face grew puzzled again.

'Never mind that. Could you be quiet for a sec? The phone's ringing.'

There was a short silence, then Hannah began speaking into the phone. 'Hello, Mrs Gordale?'

'Yes, who's that, please?'

'Mrs Gordale, this is Hannah Moore. I'm a friend of your grandson, Sam.'

'Ye-es?' The old lady's voice faltered.

'I was wondering, could I speak to Sam's mum, please?'

Silence as slowly Mrs Gordale worked it out. 'It's Carrie you want, is it?'

'Yes, please.'

'Here she is.'

Another silence, then Carrie Lawson came to the phone. 'Hello, Hannah. Nothing's wrong, I hope.'

'No, well, yes in a way . . . Don't worry, Sam's fine!' Hannah dithered.

Sam tutted and reached for the phone. He snatched it away before she could protest. 'Hello, Mum, it's me. Listen, it's about that runaway spaniel, remember?'

'Let me!' Hannah tried to grab the phone back and explain her own brilliant theory.

But Sam held tight and stormed on. 'Well, Hannah's had one of her crazy ideas. You know that fancy box of chocolates you bought for Gran? Is it still in the car?'

'Yes.' His mother sounded puzzled. 'I haven't unloaded the presents yet.'

'Could you go and check?' he asked.

'What for?'

Sam tutted and his voice had a scornful note. 'It sounds daft, but Hannah says chocolate is Samantha's favourite treat. She reckons she could've smelled them on the back seat of the car and snuck in there to eat them while no one was looking!'

'Ah!' The penny dropped. 'Wait there,' Carrie Lawson said.

'She's gone to look,' Sam whispered to the others, who held their breaths. *Maybe, just maybe* . . .

'Hello?' Mrs Lawson came back after a couple of minutes. She sounded breathless and flustered.

'Well, did you find a chocolate-covered dog?' Sam asked, as if he didn't for a moment believe in Hannah's crazy theory.

'. . . Yes!' gasped his mother.

Hannah, Helen and Laura all heard the answer loud and clear.

'. . . But!'

'But what, Mum?' Sam urged her to spit it out.

'The spaniel was there on the back seat, just like you said. There was torn wrapping everywhere, half-chewed chocolates spilling out of the box, a real mess everywhere! The strange thing is, I never noticed her all the time I was driving from Doveton to Nesfield . . .'

'Never mind that now. What we need to know is, did you manage to grab her? Have you got her somewhere safe until Laura can get across and bring her back?'

Carrie Lawson was still trying to catch her breath. She puffed and panted, then came out with the bad news. 'That's the problem. She was sitting there knowing that she'd been a naughty dog, hoping that I wouldn't notice the mess. I opened the door as carefully as I could and reached in to get a hold of her . . .'

'Oh no!' Sam groaned, guessing what was coming.

'Quick as a flash she darted forward to nip my hand, and as I snatched it away she seized her chance.'

'What happened?' Helen, Hannah and Laura cried. 'Come on, Sam, tell us!'

'She jumped down from the seat,' his mum told him, 'shot between my legs and was off down the path like greased lightning.'

'She escaped,' he said flatly.

'I'm afraid so,' Carrie said. 'And your gran's Christmas presents are ruined, all because of that sneaky little four-footed thief!'

Six

'Samantha's in Nesfield!' Laura reported back to her mother. 'What do we do now?'

'Nothing until tomorrow,' Valerie Saunders insisted.

'B-b-but!' Several voices were raised in protest.

'It's getting dark. She could freeze to death if she stays out all night!' Hannah pointed out.

'Nesfield's a big place. She'll get more and more lost!' Helen pleaded.

'And it's all my fault!' Laura was close to tears.

But nothing they could say would change Mrs Saunders' mind. 'It's not safe for you to wander around the town at night,' she explained. 'And anyway, it would be like looking for a needle in a haystack.'

Geoffrey Saunders, tall and stern as always, added his opinion. 'Your mother's right, Laura. Wait until morning.'

'That's all very well . . .' Helen muttered as she, Hannah and Sam said goodbye to Laura and made their way with Speckle up the lane. 'But how would Mr and Mrs Saunders like it if, say, Lady was stuck out in the cold?'

There was no answer to that. So they trudged silently in the grey dusk light, picturing the little black and tan dog's tiny feet pattering along dark alleys, her silky coat stiff with frost, her brown eyes glittering under the orange streetlamps.

'At least she won't starve!' Sam tried to look on the bright side at the parting of their ways. The twins stood at the gate to Home Farm, while he still had two hundred metres to walk. 'Not after she's scoffed my gran's chocolates!'

They smiled faintly.

'Are you coming to Nesfield tomorrow to help us look?' Helen asked gruffly.

'Maybe,' Sam shrugged.

'Do you want a lift with us and Mum?' Hannah knew that Mary would drive to the Curlew Cafe first thing in the morning.

'Could do.'

'Yes or no?' Helen insisted. Getting answers out of Sam was like trying to grasp hold of an eel.

'Depends,' he muttered. 'Yes, if it doesn't snow tonight. But if it does, and we all get snowed in, then none of us will be going anywhere!'

That night Helen had a dream about a cosy log fire. There were people she recognised sitting around it: their teacher, Miss Wesley; her cousin, Birdman Bates; a woman she recognised from a Diet Pepsi advert on TV . . . It was all very odd. There was a tiny Christmas tree in the corner of the room with a giant pink and silver cardboard fairy perched on top. There were crackers and balloons and everyone was laughing, except Helen herself, who found she was sitting close to the fire on a soft red velvet cushion with shiny gold tassels. 'Take it!' a voice said to her, and a hand shoved a rolled-up newspaper into her mouth. The hand belonged to Hannah but the voice was Lady Caroline's. 'Good doggy! Who's a gorgeous girl? Come to Mummy!'

Helen woke with a start to find her dad opening the bedroom curtains, peering outside and singing.

' *"Good King Wen-ces-las looked out*
On the Feast of Steph-en,
When the snow lay round about,
Deep and crisp and ev-en!" '

'Oh no! Has it snowed?' She leaped out from under the duvet with a sinking heart, almost tripping over Speckle who lay by the side of her bed. Sprinting to the window, she expected to see drifts two metres deep in the hollows of the Fell and up against the higgledy stone walls of Home Farm.

'Just a smidgeon,' David said, pointing out a light dusting of fresh, sparkling white flakes.

'Thank heavens!' Helen realised that her restless dream had been on account of her worry over Samantha. She turned to Hannah's bed, flipped off the cover and told her to get up quick.

'Uh! What time is it?' Hannah blinked and curled up into a tight ball.

'Time to go and find Samantha!'

' *". . . Brightly shone the moon that night,*

Though the frost was cru-el,
When a poor man..." '

Their dad stopped abruptly. 'Am I hearing things?' he queried, 'Or is this my daughter, Helen, expressing genuine concern about a certain pesky little pooch?'

Halfway into her clothes, Helen blushed. 'I had a dream about her,' she confessed, popping her head through the opening of her warmest jumper.

'And is this the same daughter who only yesterday refused point-blank to lift a finger to help find the said pooch?' A smile played at the corners of David Moore's mouth.

'Yeah, well – I was wrong.'

Her dad staggered and sat down on Hannah's bed. 'You hear that, Speckle? Helen just admitted she isn't perfect.'

'Da-ad!' she warned, picking up a pillow by two corners and advancing menacingly.

'Quick, fetch a pen and paper! Write it down: "I WAS WRONG!" Signed, Helen Moore!'

Bash! She swung the pillow and buffeted him sideways. *Wham*! A blow to the back of his head. *Biff*! Smack in the face.

* * *

'Feeling better, dear?' Mary asked Helen, looking in her overhead mirror as she drove the twins and Sam down to Doveton Manor so that they could pick up Laura.

They'd rushed breakfast and all their chores to be ready in time to drive to Nesfield with her. It was Christmas Eve Eve, as Hannah called it, and Mary knew that she would have a busy day at the cafe.

'I'm feeling much better, thank you!' Helen sang back at her, sitting up straight on the back seat. Her dad had begged for mercy after she'd dropped the pillow and started to tickle the soles of his bare feet. 'I've got a strong hunch that we're going to find Samantha today!'

'Me too.' Hannah was also building up her hopes, considering exactly how the four of them should plan the search.

'Good. And where will you begin?' Mary swept the car round the bend then signalled to turn into Doveton Manor.

'At Gran's house.' Sam suggested the obvious place. 'We start off where Samantha was last seen and take it from there!'

* * *

'I'm glad you lot are feeling so confident!' Laura sighed. She'd sat quietly on the journey over Hardstone Pass to Nesfield, thinking about Samantha, but now she joined in. Mary Moore had just joined a queue of slow-moving traffic into town, and was looking at her watch, wondering how long it would take to thread their way through to Mrs Gordale's house.

Sam, Hannah and Helen had been earnestly discussing tactics: first they would quiz Sam's gran, then follow up any lead she could give them. They had decided to split into two pairs; Hannah and Helen, plus Sam and Laura. That way they could cover more territory.

Hannah leaned forward to speak to Laura in the front seat. 'We really think we're going to track Samantha down,' she insisted. 'For one thing, we know exactly where she was last seen, so we can knock on people's doors and ask them if they saw which way she went. For another, it's not as if we're looking for any old breed of scruffy dog. I mean, there can't be that many black and tan Cavalier King Charles spaniels in Nesfield.'

'You're right.' Laura jutted her chin out. 'Think positive!'

'How's Lady Caroline?' Mary Moore asked, turning off the main road, down a side street and over a small hump-backed bridge.

'No better,' Laura told her. 'She didn't sleep a wink, and Mum can't get her to eat or drink anything.'

'It's a shame,' Mary sighed. She pulled up outside a tall old house with steep gables and narrow windows. There was a sign at the gate which read 'Fell View Bed and Breakfast', and another cardboard notice in the downstairs front window which told passers-by that Sam's gran had no vacancies.

Hearing their mum's cries of 'Good luck!' ringing in their ears, Hannah and Helen followed Sam up the narrow stone path. They'd never met Mrs Gordale and didn't know what to expect.

'Sammy!' she cried, opening the door as soon as he rang the bell. A small, stooping woman with curly hair dyed dark brown, large gold earrings and a lime green flowery shirt pounced on her grandson and gave him a chest-crushing hug.

Sam cringed. He escaped an even more stomach-churning kiss by ducking and twisting free in what looked to the twins like a well-rehearsed move. 'We can't stay long,' he told his grandma. 'We just need you to tell us everything you can remember about the dog in the back of Mum's car.'

'And don't I get a hug from my little Sammy first?' Mrs Gordale teased and ruffled Sam's fair hair. She obviously enjoyed seeing his face colour up bright red, as if this was all part of the game grandmothers were allowed to play.

One mega-embarrassing grandma! Helen thought. Besides the yucky hugs, her voice was too

loud, her earrings too shiny, her hairstyle too young. For the first time ever, she felt sorry for Sam Lawson.

'Gran, we want to know about the dog!' He grew more desperate. 'Did you see it run off? Which way did it go?'

'It went that-a-way!' Mrs Gordale waved her hand vaguely down the street. 'But Sammy, surely you and your little pals have time to come in for a glass of orange juice and some scrummy custard-creams!'

Hannah, Laura and Helen took a step backwards.

'Which way is that-a-way?' Sam ignored the invitation and pressed for precise directions. 'Towards the lake or away from it?'

'Away from it, dear; towards the town.' His gran gave him a reproachful look and sighed. 'You see that little snicket at the end of my row of houses? I think that's where the spaniel scarpered.'

'OK, that's where we start!' Helen was off, along the row of B and Bs, looking into each small, snowy front garden, stopping to wait for the others at the opening to the alleyway. 'It splits off in three different directions at the far end!' she warned. 'Hannah and I can follow the path to the right. Sam and Laura, you could go straight ahead.'

Only too glad to escape his grandmother's clutches, Sam agreed. 'We need a time and a place to meet up again,' he suggested, as they all set off down the alley.

'How about your gran's?' Hannah grinned.

'No, please! Let's make it your mum's cafe in half an hour.'

Everyone agreed on the Curlew. So, with a clear plan that each pair should search gardens and alleys and ask passers-by if they'd spotted a runaway Cavalier King Charles spaniel, they set off.

'. . . No, sorry, love, I haven't seen your little dog.'

'. . . Cavalier-what? What's that when it's at home?'

'. . . Black and tan . . . a little spaniel, is it? What a pity for her to get herself lost in this freezing cold weather. But no, sorry, dear, I've haven't seen hide nor hair of her.'

'How many's that?' Hannah asked, as she and Helen made their way to the Curlew. They seemed to have asked a dozen people and got the same disappointing reply.

'I don't know.' Helen's confidence that they would find Samantha was ebbing rapidly. She'd looked behind dustbins, under garden benches, even in empty greenhouses, but there wasn't a single paw-print to show where Lady Caroline's little dog had gone.

It was the same message when they met up with Sam and Laura over a mug of hot chocolate in the warm, cosy cafe.

'Zilch!' Sam reported. A white moustache of frothy cream had formed on his top lip. 'You ask people if they've seen a Cavalier King Charles spaniel and they look at you as if you're weird!'

'How can she just vanish?' Laura's face was deeply troubled and she left her hot chocolate untouched. 'I promised Lady Caroline that we'd find her!' she murmured.

'Well, I'm fed up!' Sam moaned, leaning forward to suck up more froth. 'I'm cold and bored and I wanna go home!'

No stamina! Helen thought. She was already planning the next move when her mum came over to their table.

'Laura, I just had a phone call from your father,' she said quietly. 'He guessed that at some point you would call in here. I said you were here now. He'd like to speak to you.'

Laura scraped her chair back and ran to the phone.

'Bad news?' Hannah asked Mary.

'It didn't sound too good. I think Geoffrey needs Laura back at the Manor.'

Laura confirmed this when she came back. 'Lady Caroline's worse,' she told them. 'Daddy says they have to take her to hospital in Kendal, to have her heart checked. The doctor came again, and he seems quite worried about her.'

'And they want you to go home?' Helen asked.

Laura nodded. 'The vet is due to come this afternoon to see Sultan, and on top of that, the blacksmith is coming to shoe the Shetland ponies. Everything's happening at once, and Daddy says it wouldn't do to put them off just before Christmas.'

'Quite right, you have to hold the fort,' Mary agreed. 'But how are you going to get there?'

'Taxi.' Expensive though it would be, Geoffrey Saunders had just arranged it. The driver was due any minute.

'Can I come?' Sam jumped at the chance to escape from more trudging through cold, dismal streets. He ignored the twins' hostile stares, inventing some weak excuse about having to be home to record a special TV programme on video.

'How soft can you get?' Helen muttered to Hannah.

The taxi had drawn up in the main square and Sam was scrambling in after Laura. He sank into the back seat, oblivious to their dark looks and comments.

It left only two of them to carry on the search, but Hannah wasn't going to give in. As Laura wound down the car window and leaned out, she stepped in close to reassure her. 'We'll keep on looking,' she promised.

Laura nodded. 'If you find out anything, call me.'

'Don't worry, we will.'

The dark blue car slid away from the kerb and Hannah stepped back.

'Well, girls,' Mary said, putting an arm round each of their shoulders and watching the taxi leave. 'You've set yourselves quite a task.'

'We can do it!' Helen said. *Dozens of streets, hundreds of gardens still to search*, she thought.

Hannah pictured the tiny black and tan dog cowering inside a deserted bus shelter, or shivering on the lake shore. 'Of course we can!' she agreed.

'By teatime, Samantha will be back at Doveton Manor, snoozing away like mad on her red velvet cushion!'

Seven

'Happy Christmas, girls!' Karl Thomas, the young painter and decorator who lived near the post office on Rose Terrace, had just set out to walk Samson, his Old English sheepdog, when he greeted them. 'No Speckle with you today?'

Hannah shook her head. She'd spent the last hour of fruitless searching wishing that they had brought their Border collie along. But their dad had said that Speckle deserved a rest. 'He's at home. How's Samson?'

'As full of energy as ever!' Karl let the huge dog charge along the pavement towards the twins. The shaggy sheepdog's stump of a tail wagged madly and he gave a gruff, joyful bark.

'Hello, Samson!' Helen staggered as the heavy dog jumped up and landed his front paws against her chest. She patted his woolly forehead and tried to catch her breath.

'Sorry!' Karl apologised. 'Down, Samson! I keep telling Sophie we have to get him to obedience training classes again this spring.'

'Hannah will train him for you, won't you, Hann?' Helen escaped from Samson's wet pink tongue and slyly volunteered her sister for dog-training duty.

'What? Yes, of course. But listen, Karl, you haven't seen a stray Cavalier King Charles spaniel by any chance, have you?'

'Are they the little mini ones with squished noses?' Karl held on tight to Samson as a man on a bike rode past. The dog strained at the leash and his booming bark shattered the silence of the terrace.

'No, they're the ones without squished noses. This particular one is black and tan. She ran away from Laura Saunders on Doveton Fell yesterday, sneaked a lift over to Nesfield in Sam Lawson's mum's car, then scoffed his gran's Christmas present, then—'

'Whoa!' Karl interrupted Hannah. 'I didn't see any runaway dog in town yesterday, but I've had an idea. Why not try Charles and Alice Elton?'

'Who are they?' Helen hadn't heard the name, but by this time she was willing to follow any possible lead.

'They're a couple I just did some decorating work for. They've moved into a big house on the edge of town, out near Lucy Carlton's cat sanctuary.'

'And what would they know about Samantha?' Helen couldn't make the connection.

'Maybe nothing,' Karl admitted, hauling Samson away from the edge of the pavement. 'But there's just a chance that if anyone found the kind of stray you're looking for that they would take it to the Eltons at the Evergreens.'

'But why?' It was Hannah's turn to defend herself against the Old English sheepdog's wet tongue. *Definitely more dog-training sessions for you*! she thought.

'Because they breed spaniels,' he explained. 'They've set up a boarding-kennels out there, but I hear that their main interest is in Charlies and Cavaliers. They have dozens of them, believe me!'

* * *

'This is a Tricolour Blenheim King Charles called Domino.' Alice Elton introduced Hannah and Helen to the first spaniel in a row of indoor kennels that ran down one side of a tall, airy wooden building.

The pint-sized brown, black and white spaniel looked out through a metal grille with big, soulful eyes. His little squished nose sat like a shiny black button between two floppy brown ears.

'And this is Winston.' Mrs Elton went on down the row, showing them a squat black and white dog with a big stomach and long, wavy hair. 'He needs to go on a diet and lose some weight,' the kennel owner noted.

'But what about the black and tan stray that Mr Elton found yesterday?' Hannah asked above the racket of high-pitched barks which had begun as soon as they'd walked in. Spaniels to left and right jumped up at their kennel doors, shaking their ears and pleading to be let out.

It was like the answer to a prayer; they'd said goodbye to Karl Thomas and made the long walk out of town on the Stonelea road to a modern bungalow overlooking a tiny lake. A notice at the end of the drive read 'Evergreens Boarding Kennels'. Another handwritten sign pinned to the gate said 'King Charles Pups for Sale'.

Helen and Hannah had taken their courage in both hands and knocked on the door. Alice Elton, a middle-aged woman with short grey hair, wearing a rust coloured sweater, fawn trousers and wellies, had answered it and said, yes, the twins had definitely come to the right place.

'You mean, you took in a runaway black and tan Cavalier?' Hannah had gasped. This was too good to be true. But it made sense, like Karl had said. To those who knew about it, the Evergreens would be an obvious place to bring a runaway spaniel.

'My husband, Peter, was the one who took her in,' Mrs Elton had told them, taking the girls straight through the bungalow to the kennels at the back. 'He's out there now. Let's go and find him, shall we?'

And now, neither Hannah or Helen could bear the suspense as she led them slowly down the row.

'This third one is a champion Cavalier bitch called Eugenia Ruby the Third,' Alice Elton said proudly, stopping to open the door and pick up the reddish-brown dog.

Peering ahead, Helen spotted a small, chubby man emerge from a kennel at the far end of the row. He was completely bald, with a round, shiny face and a trim white beard, dressed in a red sweater and black wellington boots. 'It's Father Christmas!' Helen whispered, then giggled.

'Shh!' Hannah speeded up. 'Excuse me, Mr Elton, we're looking for the stray dog you took in yesterday afternoon!'

'Ah, yes!' Peter Elton heard her over the din. 'A lovely little Cavalier, found wandering all alone on a busy street, about to get herself run over, by all accounts!'

'But she's OK?' Helen had caught up with Hannah and jumped in with the anxious question.

Mr Elton's shiny face creased into a smile. 'Absolutely fine. She was a bit of a mess at first; I think it was chocolate that had melted and clogged up the fur on her chest. But a good bath and towelling dry soon sorted that out.'

'And where did you say you'd found her?' Hannah asked. To their right and left, little furry dogs yelped and yapped.

'I didn't. In fact, it wasn't me who found her. A

member of the public brought her here for us to look after. He'd found her in town without a collar or any form of identification . . .'

'Are you sure?' Helen broke in. As far as she remembered, Samantha wore a neat red leather collar with a silver disc giving her name and telephone number. She glanced at Hannah and frowned.

'I suppose her collar could have caught on something and she could have tugged herself free?' Hannah said quietly. Still, she agreed with Helen; this was a bit puzzling.

'I took her in and promised to clean her up and feed her,' Peter Elton continued. 'I told the good Samaritan I knew it wouldn't be long before her owners claimed her.'

'And you were right!' Helen beamed. 'Here we are!'

Mr Elton smiled and took a squirming Eugenia Ruby the Third from his wife. The dog snuggled up against his red sweater and blinked happily at the twins. 'I'm sure you mean well and you're only trying to help,' he told them patiently. 'But if you'd spoken to Mr and Mrs Harrison earlier this morning, you could have saved yourselves the trouble of walking all the way out here!'

Helen's smile faded. Hannah began to frown. This wasn't making sense. The pieces of the jigsaw which should have fitted neatly together to allow them to take Samantha straight back home to Doveton Manor suddenly didn't fit.

'Mr and Mrs Harrison?' Hannah echoed faintly.

'Polly's owners,' Mrs Elton explained.

'Polly?' Helen gasped. She had a twisting, churning feeling in her stomach. This couldn't be right.

'Polly is the name of the runaway Cavalier.' Mr Elton stepped in to set the record straight. He looked sorry to disappoint them, but quite clear about what had happened. 'Mr and Mrs Harrison lost her over a week ago. They've been almost sick with worry about her, calling me every day to see if we'd had any news. So when the stranger brought the little scamp in yesterday afternoon, I got straight on the phone to them.'

'They say that Samantha belongs to them?' Hannah double-checked to make sure she understood. It was as if her heart had dropped through her boots; *thump*!

'No doubt about it,' Mr Elton insisted. 'They arrived within half an hour, made a big fuss of her and took her off home.'

Hannah's shoulders slumped. She felt empty and miserable. Helen made little noises of protest, but no words came out.

'So sorry to have raised your hopes, girls,' Mrs Elton said with a genuine, heartfelt sigh. 'Wouldn't it have been the perfect Christmas present if Polly had turned out to be the dog you were looking for!'

Eight

'We have to make absolutely sure!' Helen said, as soon as she recovered from her shock.

Peter and Alice Elton had been full of sympathy, offering to keep a good look out for Lady Caroline's dog over the next few days. 'Tell her we have a litter of Cavalier puppies for sale if the worst comes to the worst and she doesn't find Samantha,' Mrs Elton had said. 'Sometimes it's a good idea to replace a lost pet almost straight away, and our little pups will be ready to go to new homes soon after the New Year.'

Hannah had thanked her, but knew deep down

that this wouldn't satisfy the lonely old lady who, at this very moment, was in hospital having important tests. No, the only thing that would mend her broken heart was for them to show up with Samantha.

So she agreed now with Helen that they must check and double-check the Harrisons' story. But how?

Time was ticking on and the day was two-thirds over by the time they trudged back through slush and ice to the town square in Nesfield. Though it was tempting to call in at the Curlew for another cup of chocolate, instead they gave their mum a wave through the window, and decided to carry on with their detective work.

'You know what bothers me?' Hannah muttered, as Helen had a brainwave and darted into the post office to flick through the telephone directory. 'Mr Elton mentioned that the stray dog was messy when she was brought in, and that the stuff she was covered in was melted chocolate!'

Helen nodded eagerly, running her finger down the long list of Harrises then on to Harrisons. 'Which makes it the same dog as the one that Sam's mum found on the back seat of her car . . . which also means that it must be Samantha!' Once her brain got working again, she grew more and more convinced that the Eltons had made a terrible mistake in handing over the dog.

'I mean, these Harrisons could be like Danny Jones!' Hannah went on. 'You remember when we found Speckle dumped in the quarry and he claimed he belonged to him!'

'Of course I remember!' Helen pinpointed three Harrisons who lived in Nesfield, pulled a pen and a scrap of paper from her pocket and wrote down all three names and addresses.

'They could be lying through their teeth!' Hannah grew angry at the very idea. 'When Mr Elton phoned them and they went to Evergreens, they could've already decided that whatever happened they were going to say that the dog belonged to them!'

'Yeah, yeah, I know!' Helen showed her the addresses. 'Which one do we try first?'

'The nearest.'

'That's this one.' Helen stabbed her finger at the address which read 23 Bridge Street, then stepped out across the square. She recognised Bridge Street as the road which ran alongside the river running into Rydal Lake; it was only a few hundred metres away and they could be there in under five minutes.

But when they arrived, they found there was no one in at number 23. Then a woman bringing in shopping from her car into the house next door asked Helen and Hannah what they wanted and told them that her neighbours, the Harrisons, didn't have, had *never* had and never *would* have a Cavalier King Charles spaniel.

'Why not?' Hannah asked. She felt a dead-end looming.

'Because they have a little boy, Nathan, and he has asthma. Dogs and cats set off an attack if they come within ten metres of him. That's why they can't have pets.'

Yep; a big brick wall, Hannah thought.

But Helen had another question for the busy, chatty neighbour. 'Do Mr Harrison's parents live in Nesfield?'

'Yes, as a matter of fact they live just down the road on River Street.' The woman stopped on her doorstep and gave Helen a curious glance.

'And they wouldn't have a spaniel either, would they?'

'How do you work that out?'

'Because if they had a dog, their grandson wouldn't be able to visit them, would he?'

'Right!' The neighbour nodded approvingly at Helen's quick thinking. Then she took herself and her carrier-bags through her front door, which closed with a firm click of the latch.

'Well done, Helen!' Excitedly Hannah took the list and crossed off both Bridge Street and River Street. 'That only leaves the Harrisons at the Shepherd's Dog, Hardstone Road!'

'Which is way out of town!' Helen sighed wearily.

But Hannah wouldn't let her flag. She set off at a rapid pace, knowing that the daylight would give out on them by four o'clock at the latest. That gave them just over two hours to check out the people who had claimed the dog.

'It's all uphill!' Helen complained half an hour later. The backs of her legs ached, and despite the Christmas tree lights winking in the windows of the cottages that they'd passed, she herself was feeling distinctly un-Christmassy. She would give a lot, she thought, to be back home finishing her cards or volunteering to make mince-pies.

'Nearly there!' Hannah had remembered that the Shepherd's Dog was in fact a small, old-fashioned pub standing at a bend in the road where the town became country, just before the narrow, winding road over Hardstone Pass began in earnest. They passed the old stone building every time they drove that way, yet she had never paid it any attention, except to notice that the pub sign showed a picture of a black and white Border collie that looked like their very own Speckle. 'Here it is now!' she cried as they came over the brow of the hill.

Helen's pace picked up and her face set in more determined lines. 'OK!' she said through gritted teeth. 'This is it!'

Hannah too marched on, prepared for a confrontation. In her mind's eye she saw the Harrisons as a shady pair running a scruffy pub that smelt of stale beer and cigarette smoke. They would be big and fat. He would need a shave and would probably be wearing a worn string vest under a dirty open-necked shirt. She would be in laddered tights and worn-out slippers, and Hannah wouldn't be surprised if she even had those old-fashioned curler things in her straggly grey hair.

'Ready?' Helen reached the door of the pub and hesitated. The middle of the afternoon on Christmas Eve Eve didn't seem a good time for two girls to be going into what looked like an empty pub. True, there were cheery Christmas lights at the window and a gleaming white Morris Traveller polished to perfection standing outside the door, which gave the place a well-kept air. But still . . .

'Ready!' Hannah said, taking the lead. She thought of that moment when they went back to Doveton Manor with Samantha safe in their arms . . .

There were shiny copper warming-pans on the white walls, gleaming brass lanterns hanging from a beamed ceiling. Rows of spotless glasses stood on shelves behind the bar, whose dark wooden surface was clean and polished. The red, patterned carpet was freshly hoovered; the beaten-copper tables around the room shone like mirrors.

And on a red cushion by the fire in a far corner slept a small black and tan dog.

'Can I help you?' the landlord asked, coming out from a room behind the bar. He was small and neat, and somehow as shiny and old fashioned as everything else in the bar.

Helen and Hannah stared hard at the sleeping dog.

'What d'you think?' Helen hissed.

Hannah shrugged and shook her head.

'Now I don't think you two are eighteen,' the old man said, 'so I can't serve you anything alcoholic!' Smiling at his own little jest, he came out from behind the bar.

No string vest, Hannah noted, and no unsightly stubble. If this was Mr Harrison, he wasn't at all what she'd been expecting. This man in his fawn hand-knitted cardigan and crisp khaki-green collar and tie was no Danny Jones.

'We . . . we came about the dog,' Helen stammered.

As if realising what she had said, the black and tan spaniel opened her eyes and lifted her head.

'Oh, you can't believe how pleased we are to have Polly back!' Mr Harrison launched straight into the happy story of how they'd found their long-lost pet. 'To be honest with you, my wife, Christine, and I regard it as a little Christmas miracle! We'd just about given up hope!'

The dog – Samantha or Polly? – opened her mouth, yawned and rolled on to her side, from which position she stretched her legs over the edge of the worn red cushion and lazily wagged her flag-like, feathery tail.

'Are you sure . . . erm . . . can you prove . . . that is . . . ?' Hannah faltered and faded.

'Mr and Mrs Elton told us you'd claimed the dog,' Helen said lamely, before she too tailed off.

'Christine says it's a real godsend, the perfect Christmas present to have Polly back with us.' The old man didn't seem to notice the twins' confusion. Instead, he beckoned them over to take a closer look at the spaniel.

And as they gingerly crossed the carpet so as not to startle her, Mrs Harrison appeared out of the back room, teatowel in hand. She was taller than her husband, but equally shiny. Her glasses had fancy silver frames which reflected the firelight, she wore a gold brooch and gold necklaces, her white blouse had a satiny sheen.

No curlers. Hannah grimaced. This was getting worse by the second; Mr and Mrs Harrison actually seemed really nice!

'Do you girls like Cavaliers?' Christine Harrison asked brightly, folding her teatowel and putting it down on the bar. 'Did you see the gorgeous little puppies at the Evergreens? We're thinking of having one ourselves after Christmas, even though we've got Polly back; and thank heavens for that!'

'Hm!' Hannah grunted, stopping a few feet away from the dog on the cushion. She could feel the glow of the fire burning her cheeks, and her heart thumping awkwardly at the situation they'd got themselves into.

'They're such friendly, obedient little dogs,' Mrs Harrison went on, oblivious. 'They have such happy temperaments; never a cross word!'

'Helen!' Hannah whispered as Mr Harrison stood to one side to let his wife bend down and speak to the spaniel. 'This is it! This is the proof we need!'

'What is?' Helen mumbled out of the corner of her mouth.

'. . . Yes, you're a gorgeous girl, aren't you, Polly? You understand every word we say!' The landlady cooed and crowed over her much-loved dog.

'Don't you see?' Hannah hissed. 'Samantha never obeyed an order in her entire life. I'm gonna see if I can get Mrs Harrison to tell her to do something;

she's bound to ignore her or even bite her ankle with a bit of luck!'

'In which case, we can tell them that this isn't Polly!' Hannah saw the point. 'OK, fingers crossed!' she agreed.

'Erm, Mrs Harrison, can Sam – er – Polly do any tricks?' Hannah asked, holding her breath for the reply.

'She can indeed. She can fetch Frank's slippers from the back room and put them down at his feet if I just say one word!' the landlady said proudly.

'Could she do it now?' Hannah ventured.

Christine Harrison smiled and raised her forefinger to catch the spaniel's attention.

The dog sat up, ears pricked, head cocked to one side.

'Polly, fetch!' Mrs Harrison said.

The dog stood up and padded across the carpet. She disappeared behind the bar. Five seconds later, she reappeared carrying one large, soft and rather battered brown leather slipper.

'Good girl, Polly!' Mrs Harrison beamed. 'Now, drop!'

Half dragging, half carrying the slipper, the spaniel

took it right up to Mr Harrison and placed it neatly at his feet.

Hannah's eyes opened wide with dismay. Helen's forehead was creased with disappointment.

'You see!' Mr Harrison cried. 'She's the perfect dog. She eats whatever you put in front of her, no fuss. She even goes out with me in all weathers and walks down the hill to collect the paper from the newsagent's, carries it all the way back up without so much as making a mark on it!'

How could this be? How was it possible? Stunned into silence, the twins backed off towards the door.

'I could've sworn . . . !' Hannah whispered.

'Me too!' Helen agreed.

This dog was the same size, she had the same black body and bright tan chest. There were identical markings over her eyes and on the insides of her long, floppy ears.

But this one fetched and carried, did exactly as she was told.

No; they must have been wrong. This couldn't be Samantha-Henrietta-Tansy of Fife after all.

Or could it?

As the spaniel deposited her master's slipper and wagged her tail, waiting no doubt for a treat as a reward, she happened to give Helen and Hannah a sideways look.

Mr and Mrs Harrison didn't see it; they were too busy searching in their pockets for a doggy choc to notice. But the girls did. It was a look quite out of character for angelic Polly; a curl of the lip into a slight snarl, a flash of pointed white teeth that could nip and hurt.

And in her eye was an intense warning signal that they later described as, *Don't you dare give the game away*!

'. . . It *is* Samantha!' Helen insisted, as they ran out of the pub and back down the hill. 'It's so – so *her*!'

'But how do we prove it?' Hannah asked. She slowed to a walk and cast around helplessly, looking up to the grey, darkening sky for a solution to the impossible problem. 'And if we do prove it, just think what it would do to poor Mr and Mrs Harrison!'

Nine

Lady Caroline had had the tests at the hospital and was back at Doveton Manor by the time Hannah and Helen got a lift back with their mum.

Mary Moore had offered her thoughts on the Polly-Samantha problem as they drove past the Shepherd's Dog and Helen had filled her in.

'The thing is, Mr and Mrs Harrison totally believe that it's their dog,' she'd explained. 'But Hannah and me think she's only pretending to be Polly!'

'That would take a pretty clever dog,' Mary had pointed out. 'You mean, Samantha's pretending to be angelic so that she can be mistaken for Polly and gets to stay with Mr and Mrs Perfect Owner?'

Hannah had tried to convince her it was true by reminding their mum about the sticky chocolate mess that the Eltons had had to clean off the stray dog's chest.

'Could be coincidence.' Mary had driven over the pass, down into Doveton, still unconvinced. 'And you know the main reason why I'm doubtful about your theory?' she'd asked, stopping at the Manor gates to let the twins out.

'No one ever believes us!' Helen had wailed.

'It's true, Mum!' Hannah had pleaded.

But Mary Moore had stuck to her guns. 'Listen, the main reason is this fetching and carrying of slippers thing. You've said yourselves that Lady Caroline's dog is the most disobedient creature you've ever come across, so how on earth would it be possible for Samantha to pick up the slipper trick so quickly – in less than twenty four hours, in fact?'

Neither Helen nor Hannah could come up with an answer. So Mary had advised them not to even mention their visit to the pub when they called in at Doveton Manor.

'Not even to Laura?' Hannah had asked.

'Not a word to anyone. It would only raise false hopes.' Mary had said goodbye and driven on up the lane.

And anyway, the Saunderses were so worried about their Scottish guest that it was easy at first for the twins to avoid the subject of their visit to the Harrisons' pub.

'She's pining for Samantha,' Valerie Saunders said sadly. 'It turns out that Caroline has a history of heart problems; a slight murmur was detected many years ago and the doctors have always said that she should try to avoid stress. But in fact it's been a horrid year for her, what with Sir Anthony dying suddenly. So it's no wonder that Samantha's disappearance has hit her so badly . . .'

'Uh-hum!' From the door of the kitchen where Helen, Hannah, Laura and Valerie had gathered, Geoffrey Saunders made a stagey throat-clearing noise.

The conversation stopped short and Lady Caroline herself came up beside Laura's father.

'I know that you were discussing me!' the old lady said with a wry smile. 'In fact, my ears were burning as I came down the stairs!'

Hannah and Helen smiled back awkwardly. They saw how pale Lady Caroline looked, and spotted a slight tremble in her hands as she came slowly into the kitchen. Though she was tall and dignified-looking with her cropped grey hair and heather-coloured cardigan and tweed skirt, she was also much more frail and sad than they'd noticed before.

'I hear you've spent the day searching for my poor little dog?' she said, fixing the twins with her anxious stare. 'Did you manage to pick up any clues?'

'No, sorry!' Hannah said abruptly.

'Not really!' Helen said over the top of Hannah.

Then they both coughed and shuffled and looked away.

'The trail went cold after we all left Sam Lawson's gran's house,' Laura explained.

Lady Caroline sighed and drifted away from the disappointing news into memories of how life had been when Sir Anthony was alive. 'Samantha absolutely adored my husband! And he was so sweet with her. He used to teach her all sorts of clever little tricks!' Her hand fingered a gold locket which she wore on a chain around her neck. 'I have pictures of the two of them in here; my favourite photographs. Would you like to see?'

'Erm . . .' Hannah was ready to back away and dash off to Home Farm. This history of the Urquharts was getting too sad for her to listen to.

But Helen jumped at the chance. 'Yes, please. I'd love to look!' She waited impatiently as Lady Caroline's shaking fingers prised the locket open, then she peered closly at the two tiny photographs. '. . . Brilliant!' she said after a long pause.

'You like them?' The old lady seemed pleased.

'Hann, come and look at this!' Helen cried excitedly. 'Samantha's doing an interesting trick!'

'What is it?' Hannah edged forward to study the photograph on the left hand side of the locket. It seemed to be of a tall man with a moustache, wearing a tartan kilt, standing beside a bright log fire. In the photo on the right Samantha was sitting to attention, holding something in her mouth . . . And that something (there was no doubt about it when she looked even more closely) was a well worn brown leather slipper!

'So that explains how come the dog at the pub was so good on the fetch-the-slipper routine!'

Helen gabbled at her mum and dad the moment
she flew through the door to find them hanging
tinsel from a tree which her dad had bought that
afternoon.

'She didn't have to be taught from scratch!'
Hannah explained. 'She already knew how to do
it!'

'*If – if – if*!' David was standing on a stool, trying
to loop trimmings over the upper branches of the
prickly tree. 'You're putting an awful lot of maybes
into the situation.'

'No, we're not!' Helen protested. 'We've worked

it out really carefully. And we're one hundred per cent sure that the dog we saw this afternoon is Samantha!'

For a few moments, as Helen and Hannah hopped and fidgeted impatiently round the kitchen, their mum and dad went on decorating the tree.

'Say you're right,' Mary began in her most down-to-earth voice. 'How come Mr and Mrs Harrison haven't spotted the difference between their own dog and someone else's?'

'Good point!' David mumbled, strands of tinsel clenched between his teeth. He wobbled on the stool as he reached round the back. 'Ouch!' The sharp needles pricked his bare arms.

'Hmm.' Helen hadn't got a reason ready.

'Easy!' Hannah came in with an answer. 'I was wondering about that, and what I think is, Cavalier King Charles spaniels are pedigrees, which means they're all inbred to make them fit the breed description. You know; they all have their eyes set wide apart, their ears are long and feathery, they have a short body and a springy walk . . .'

Slowly Mary and David stopped what they were doing and turned to stare at their well-informed daughter.

'I looked it up in a book.' She blushed. 'Anyway, all black and tan Cavaliers have to have the same pattern of markings, down to the little tan blotches over their eyes.'

'In other words, they all look exactly the same!' Helen breathed, her eyes gleaming.

Hannah nodded. 'So that's how the Harrisons made the mistake. That, and the fact that they must really really have *wanted* the dog at the Evergreens to be Polly! So they kind of persuaded themselves that it must be!'

David looked down open-mouthed from the height of his stool. 'Frightening!' he whispered. 'The girl's a genius!'

Mary nodded. 'OK, you win!' she admitted to the twins. 'It looks pretty likely that Samantha has ended up with the wrong owners.'

'Yes!' Hannah and Helen clenched their fists in victory salutes.

'But!' Mary warned. 'Have you really got the heart to go back to the pub and tell these kind-hearted people that Polly isn't Polly after all, and that you've come to take her away?'

Hannah swallowed hard. Helen frowned and bit her lip.

'And!' Mary went on. 'Is it such a good thing to let Lady Caroline take Samantha back to her castle in Scotland to let her lead a spoiled life of luxury, when she could live a contented, ordinary, even useful life with the Harrisons?'

'But Lady Caroline could learn *not* to spoil her,' Hannah argued. 'Samantha hasn't always been a snobby little pest; not when Sir Anthony was alive!'

'Yeah,' Helen agreed. She was torn this way and that. 'But what about the Harrisons?'

Hannah had to think hard about this one. Genius or not, the solution wasn't obvious. Then, 'I know!' she said at last. It had come in a blinding flash; the simple answer.

'What?' her mum and dad and Helen chorused.

'We have to find the real Polly!' she said. 'And then everyone will be happy!'

Ten

'They just forecast more snow. It looks like it's going to be a white Christmas.' David Moore handed Helen and Hannah their scarves and hats. 'Now, if it does start while you're out looking for the mysterious vanishing Polly, you must head straight back to the cafe and wait there until it stops, you hear?'

'Da-ad!' Hannah tutted as she wound her scarf around her neck. It was Christmas Eve; the last possible day for her and Helen to wave their magic wands. They had to find the original missing spaniel, take her back to the Harrisons, collect Samantha and deliver her to Lady Caroline. A tall order, but she was sure they could do it. 'A little bit of snow won't hurt us!'

'Promise!' he insisted.

'OK.' Helen agreed to be sensible. Looking out of the window at the heavy grey clouds over Doveton Fell, she reckoned that the forecasters could be right.

'Ready?' Mary scooted through the kitchen collecting her bag, her keys, her gloves and a can of de-icer for the car windscreen.

'Yep!' The girls were out of the door before her, dashing so fast that they almost bumped in to Sam Lawson, who was standing on the doorstep.

Sam lost his balance and juggled a flat, square parcel wrapped in silver paper and tied with red ribbon. It tipped and fell, but he moved to catch it before it hit the ground.

'Howzat!' David grinned and applauded the catch. 'What brings you here so early, Sam?'

'I need a lift into Nesfield, if that's OK with you, Mrs Moore.'

'Fine. Climb in.' Mary hardly paused in her rush to get to work.

'Hey, let me guess what's in the parcel!' Helen plonked herself in the back seat and watched him get in. 'More chocolates for your gran!'

'Right,' he grunted. 'Mum sent me to see if I could drive over with your mum to save her the journey. She wanted Gran to have her present in time for Christmas Day.'

'Well, we're on Spaniel Hunt Number Two!' Hannah explained the latest developments. 'What are you doing after you've dropped off the chocs?'

'Nothing much.' Sam shrugged and gazed vaguely out of the window.

'We-ell . . .' Needing all the help they could get, Helen used her arts of persuasion. 'If you joined in with us, that would mean you wouldn't have to stay long at your gran's house, wouldn't it?'

'Say no more!' he shot back, suddenly paying attention. 'Count me in. And I can tell Gran we don't have a minute to lose!'

'Sammy!' Mrs Gordale's face lit up as she took the silver parcel from her grandson. 'Oh, lovey, you shouldn't have gone to all this trouble!'

Sam dodged as she leaned forward to hug him. 'Can't stay, Gran. Gotta go!'

'But what's the hurry? Don't you and your little

friends want to come in and get warm?'

'No thanks!' Helen cried.

'We haven't got time!' Hannah gasped.

Mrs Gordale hugged the wrapped box of chocolates to her chest as if it was a delightful secret. 'Are you sure?' she purred.

'Gran, we're looking for a dog!' Sam said hurriedly, refusing to step foot over the doorstep.

'Yes, I know you are.' She winked and smiled. 'Why don't you come in? I may have something interesting to show you.'

'No, not that dog, Gran. A different one. Well, the same kind of dog, actually . . . but not the same dog . . . !' Exasperated, Sam's tongue and brain both got into a twist.

'Oh, Sammy, sometimes you do talk nonsense!' By this time, Mrs Gordale was beaming from earring to earring. 'Listen, dear, I know you're trying to track down that little scamp who ate my first box of chocolates . . .'

'No!' Hannah began. But she was silenced by an energetic wave of Mrs Gordale's hand.

. . . And I was going to ring you at home as soon as I'd had my breakfast,' she went on, ushering them into the narrow hallway. 'So your coming here in person is just one of those little Christmas miracles that keep on happening.'

Sam fell over his feet and came up against a glass table loaded with china ornaments. Hannah and Helen steadied him before he crashed into it. 'What's going on?' he demanded.

Mrs Gordale bustled them down the corridor towards her kitchen at the back of the house. 'I feel like a fairy godmother!' she cooed. 'Only, it's not quite, "Cinderella, you *shall* go to the ball!" It's more, "Children, you *shall* find your runaway dog!" '

Helen and Hannah tripped and stumbled behind Sam, who kept on turning to demand an explanation. They glanced at each other, completely baffled.

'My neighbour across the road, Mrs Hebden, just happened to come out on to her doorstep to collect her milk when I opened my door for the Christmas post.' Mrs Gordale chatted as she hustled. 'She gave me a shout. She said, "Mrs Gordale, did I hear that your grandson and his friends were looking for a little black and tan spaniel?" I said yes, that was quite correct. She said, "Look no further!" And so, it turns out that the little pest who stole my choccies didn't run far after all!'

Sam had reached the kitchen door and stopped point-blank. Helen and Hannah cannoned into him. They huddled into a corner to let Sam's gran sweep past.

'And lo!' she said, pushing the door open and inviting them in. 'Guess who managed to get herself locked in Mrs Hebden's nasty dark shed at the bottom of her long, cold garden?'

'Polly!' Hannah gasped.

A black and tan Cavalier lay large as life on the tiled floor in Mrs Gordale's empty picnic basket. The basket was padded with a soft checked blanket, the spaniel was resting, head on paws with a quizzical look, blinking up at her astonished visitors.

'So, you see, she's pretty thin after more than a week of being trapped in the shed,' Hannah told Christine Harrison. 'There was a leak in the roof, which meant she was able to drink the melting snow as it dripped through the crack. But the only thing to eat was a bag of old rabbit food on a low shelf. It kept her from starving, though.'

The plan had been for Helen and Sam to wait

outside the Shepherd's Dog with Polly, so as not to burst in on the Harrisons with too much of a surprise. It had been Hannah's job to go ahead into the bar and offer the kindly couple a slow, gentle explanation.

'Let me get this straight,' Frank Harrison said. 'There are two identical Cavalier King Charles spaniels, and they both ran away. The one we have on this cushion by the fire isn't our Polly; it's a dog we never set eyes on before!'

Hannah nodded hard. 'If you think about it, wasn't this one a bit too sleek and well-fed when you picked her up at the Evergreens? Wouldn't Polly have been a lot thinner and scraggier after a week on the run?'

'B-but!' Mrs Harrison was finding it hard to come to terms with what Hannah was telling them. 'She greeted us as if she'd known us all her life . . . And, and, she even feched Frank's slippers for him!'

'Ah well, Samantha would know when she was on to a good thing,' Hannah told them, looking sternly at the pampered pooch on the cushion. 'She's pretty smart.'

Samantha stared back wide-eyed and innocent.

'Would you like to see the dog that was found in Mrs Hebden's shed?' Hannah asked politely. She didn't want to push the Harrisons too hard.

Frank glanced at his wife, then nodded. 'Bring her in.'

So Hannah opened the door for Helen to carry in the little dog still wrapped in Mrs Gordale's checked red and black blanket. Sam followed quietly behind.

'Here she is,' Helen said.

The tiny spaniel peeped out of the blanket at the polished tables and bright log fire. She took in the rows of glasses and the amazed landlords staring at her dumbfounded.

Helen felt the little dog's tail begin to wag, saw her floppy ears prick up. She unwrapped the blanket and set her carefully on the carpet.

'*Woof*!' Polly saw that an invader had plonked herself on her very own cushion. Her hackles raised, she bared her sharp little teeth and, scraggy and thin as she was, she made a bee-line for Samantha.

'*Mmm-nnn*!' Samantha whined. The game was up. Down went her head and she crept off the cushion. '*Mm-mm-mmm*!' She skulked across the room, dragging her tail, saying '*Sorry, sorry, sorry! Don't tell me off. After all, what would you have done if you'd been me?*'

The overjoyed Harrisons had thanked Hannah and Helen over and over, then offered them a reward.

'Anything you like!' Christine had said, hugging Polly close. 'We can't thank you enough and we'd like to make your Christmas as happy as ours is going to be now that we have the real Polly back!'

Hannah had quickly taken pity on the whining Samantha and picked her up. She'd done a swift, secret calculation, plucked up courage and requested what sounded to her like an enormous sum. 'Would £5 be too much?' she'd asked nervously.

No sooner said than done. Frank Harrison had produced the note from his pocket and told them to buy themselves a nice Christmas treat.

Then they were off with Samantha wrapped in the blanket, out into the cold morning, wondering how they were going to get over to Doveton with the good news.

'Watch out, here comes another fairy godmother!' Helen grinned as she saw Fred Hunt's Land Rover chug up the hill out of town.

Sam flagged him down for a lift.

'Why all the giggles and funny looks?' the old farmer asked as they climbed in.

'Nothing!' Hannah assured him. Was this turning out perfectly, or what?

' "You *shall* go to Doveton Manor!" ' Helen cried, tumbling into the back of the Land Rover and pretending to wave an imaginary wand.

'Samantha; my very own Samantha!' Lady Caroline's eyes were full of tears. Her hands trembled, not with worry but with overflowing gratitude.

The little group of relieved searchers stood with Laura in the spacious living-room at Doveton Manor.

'Well done!' Laura whispered. 'This is absolutely brilliant!' As yet, she didn't understand how it had happened; all she knew was that their guest was happy at last.

And they could all see that little Samantha was almost beside herself with excitement. She cuddled against her owner, reaching up to lick her chin, paddling her paws against her mauve twinset. Her long tail wagged rhythmically to and fro.

'I promise never, never to let you get lost again!' Lady Caroline hugged and squeezed. 'And I'm going to be very strict with you from now on, so you won't be able to get away with all those naughty little things you've been doing lately!'

Good move! Hannah thought.

Helen gave a look that said, *Dream on*!

'I mean it!' the old lady said in a mock-severe voice. 'No more jumping up, no more nipping people, do you hear?'

Samantha put her head to one side and gave a worried whimper. *What's this? Are you threatening to turn over a new leaf*?

'Yes, that's right!' Lady Caroline sounded quite determined as she looked round the room with a radiant smile. 'And it's for your own good. When I get you home to Fife, I'm going to turn you back into the lovely, obedient, friendly little dog that I know and love!'

'*Woof*!' *We'll see*! Samantha wriggled free, jumped to the floor and trotted swiftly towards her red tasselled cushion. She lay down by the fire and contentedly licked her paws.

'Do you think Lady Caroline *will* teach Samantha to be good again?' Helen asked.

She and Hannah lay in the dark, trying in vain to get to sleep.

'Yep.' Hannah sounded confident. 'I'm gonna lend her my *Two Weeks to a Perfectly Trained Dog*. She can read it over the New Year.'

'Hmm.' Helen listened out for the arrival of their Christmas presents. It was the same each year; she would want to stay awake to investigate, but never quite make it. In the morning, the stocking at the foot of the bed would be filled as if by magic. '. . . Hann?' she whispered.

'Hmmm?'

'What did you buy with that £5 from Mr Harrison?'

She'd been too busy to ask at the time, on the way through Doveton, when Hannah had handed Samantha to her while Fred stopped at Luke Martin's shop and she'd popped inside with him.

'I thought you'd never ask!' Hannah sprang out of her bed and tunnelled underneath, dragging out a carefully wrapped parcel shaped like a small treasure chest. 'For Mum!' she hissed. 'A surprise!'

Helen slid out from under her duvet and knelt beside Hannah. She took the parcel and shook it, listened carefully, shook it again. 'What is it?'

'Guess!' Hannah's brown eyes shone in the starlight.

'Belgian chocolates!' Helen had a brainwave and knew she'd guessed right even before Hannah nodded.

'Do you think she'll like them?'

Helen grinned. 'She'll love 'em! And so will we!'

They slid the parcel back under the bed and snuck under their covers.

'Happy Christmas, Hann,' Helen said sleepily.

'Yeah . . . Happy Christmas,' Hannah replied, falling asleep at last.